Bedtime Stories

Stories in This Book

THORNTON W. BURGESS
Bedtime Stories

Illustrated by CARL and MARY HAUGE

GROSSET & DUNLAP · Publishers · NEW YORK
A FILMWAYS COMPANY

1978 Printing
ISBN: 0-448-02874-3 (Trade Edition)
ISBN: 0-448-12690-7 (Paperback Edition)
ISBN: 0-448-03326-0 (Library Edition)
Library of Congress Catalog Card Number: 76-14691

Buster Bear Goes Fishing

BUSTER BEAR yawned as he lay on his comfortable bed of leaves and watched the first early morning sunbeams creeping through the Green Forest to chase out the Black Shadows.

"I'm going fishing," said he in his deep grumbly-rumbly voice to no one in particular. "Yes, Sir, I'm going fishing. I want some fat trout for my breakfast."

He shuffled along over to the Laughing Brook, and straight to a little pool of which he knew. Now it just happened that, early as he was, someone was before Buster Bear. When he came in sight of the little pool, whom should he see but another fisherman there, who had already caught a fine fat trout. Who was it?

From *The Adventures of Buster Bear*, Copyright, 1916, 1944, by Thornton W. Burgess.

Why, Little Joe Otter, to be sure. He was just climbing up the bank with the fat trout in his mouth. Buster Bear's own mouth watered as he saw it. Little Joe sat down on the bank and prepared to enjoy his breakfast. He hadn't seen Buster Bear, and he didn't know that he or anyone else was anywhere near.

Buster Bear tiptoed up very softly until he was right behind Little Joe Otter. "Woof, woof!" said he in his deepest, most grumbly-rumbly voice.

Little Joe Otter gave a frightened squeal and without even turning to see who was speaking dropped his fish and dived headfirst into the Laughing Brook. Buster Bear sprang forward and with one of his big paws caught the fat trout just as it was slipping back into the water.

"Here's your trout, Mr. Otter," said he, as Little Joe put his head out of water to see who had frightened him so. "Come and get it."

But Little Joe wouldn't. The fact is, he was afraid to. He snarled at Buster Bear and called him a thief and everything bad he could think of. Buster didn't seem to mind. He chuckled as if he thought it all a great joke and repeated his invitation to Little Joe to come and get his fish. But Little Joe just turned his back and went off down the Laughing Brook in a great rage.

"It's too bad to waste such a fine fish," said Buster thoughtfully. "I wonder what I'd better do with it." And while he was wondering, he ate it all up. Then he started down the Laughing Brook to try to catch some for himself.

Little Joe Otter was in a terrible rage. "I was sitting on the bank of the Laughing Brook beside one of the little pools," he told Billy Mink, "and was just going to eat a fat trout I had caught, when who should come along but that great big bully, Buster Bear. He took that fat trout away from me and ate it just as if it belonged to him! I hate him! If I live long enough I'm going to get even with him!"

Of course, that wasn't nice talk, and anything but a nice spirit, but Little Joe Otter's temper is sometimes pretty short, especially when he is hungry, and this time he had had no breakfast, you know.

Buster Bear hadn't actually taken the fish away from Little Joe. But looking at the matter as Little Joe did, it amounted to the same thing. You see, Buster knew perfectly well when he invited Little Joe to come back and get it that Little Joe wouldn't dare do anything of the kind.

"Where is he now?" asked Billy Mink.

"He's somewhere up the Laughing Brook."

"Let's go see what he is doing," said Billy Mink.

At first Little Joe didn't want to, but at last his curiosity got the better of his fear, and he agreed. So the two little brown-coated scamps turned down the Laughing Brook, taking the greatest care to keep out of sight themselves. They had gone only a little way when Billy Mink whispered, "Sh-h! There he is."

"What's he doing?" asked Little Joe Otter, as Buster Bear sat for the longest time without moving.

Just then one of Buster's big paws went into the water as quick as a flash and scooped out a trout that had ventured too near.

"He's fishing!" exclaimed Billy Mink.

"They are our fish!" said Little Joe fiercely. "He has no business catching our fish!"

"I don't see how we are going to stop him," said Billy Mink.

"I do!" cried Little Joe, into whose head an idea had just popped. "Just you watch me get even with Buster Bear."

Little Joe slipped swiftly into the water and swam straight to the little pool that Buster would try next. He frightened the fish so that they fled in every direction. Then he stirred up the mud until the water was so dirty that Buster couldn't have seen a fish right under his nose. He did the same thing in the next pool and the next. Buster Bear's fishing was spoiled for that day.

Chatterer the Red Squirrel Learns a Lesson

CHATTERER the Red Squirrel had been scolding because there was no excitement. He had even tried to make some excitement by waking Bobby Coon and making him so angry that Bobby had threatened to eat him alive. It had been great fun to dance around and call Bobby names and make fun of him. Oh, yes, it had been great fun. You see, he knew all the time that Bobby couldn't catch him if he should try. But now things were different. Chatterer had all the excitement that he wanted. Indeed, he had more than he wanted. The truth is, Chatterer was running for his life, and he knew it.

It was Shadow the Weasel from whom Chatterer was running, and Shadow is so slim that he can slip in and out of places that even Chatterer cannot get through.

From *The Adventures of Chatterer the Red Squirrel,* Copyright, 1915, 1943, by Thornton W. Burgess.

"Oh, dear! Oh, dear!" he sobbed, as he ran out on the branch of a tree and leaped across to the next tree. "I wish I had minded my own business! I wish I had kept my tongue still. Shadow the Weasel wouldn't have known where I was if he hadn't heard my voice. Oh, dear! Oh, dear me! What can I do?"

Suddenly Chatterer saw a big brown bunch near the top of a tall chestnut tree, and he headed for that tree as fast as ever he could go. What was that big brown bunch? Why, it was Redtail the Hawk, who was dozing there with his head drawn down between his shoulders, dreaming.

Now old Redtail is one of Chatterer's deadliest enemies. He is quite as fond of Red Squirrel as is Shadow the Weasel, though he doesn't often try to catch one, because there are other things to eat much easier to get. Chatterer had had more than one narrow escape from old Redtail and was very much afraid of him, yet here he was running up the very tree in which Redtail was sitting. You see, a very daring idea had come into his head. He had seen at once that Redtail was dozing and hadn't seen him at all. He knew that Redtail would just as soon have Shadow the Weasel for dinner as himself, and a daring plan popped into his head.

"I may as well be caught by Redtail as Shadow," he thought, as he ran up the tree, "but if my plan works out right, I won't be caught by either. Anyway, it is my very last chance."

Up the tree he scrambled, and after him went Shadow the Weasel. Shadow had been so intent on catching Chatterer that he had not noticed old Redtail, which was just as Chatterer had hoped. Up, up he scrambled, straight past old Redtail, but as he passed, he pulled one of Redtail's long tail feathers, and then ran on to the top of the tree, and with the last bit of strength he had left, leaped to a neighboring spruce tree where, hidden by the thick branches, he stopped to rest and see what would happen.

Of course, when he felt his tail pulled, old Redtail was wide awake in a flash; and of course he looked down to see who had dared to pull his tail. There just below him was Shadow the Weasel, who had just that minute discovered who was sitting there. Old Redtail hissed sharply, and the feathers on the top of his head stood up in a way they do when he is angry. And he was angry — very angry.

Shadow the Weasel stopped short. Then, like a flash, he dodged around to the other side of the tree. He had no thought of Chatterer now. Things were changed all in an instant, quite changed. Instead of the hunter, he was now the hunted. Old Redtail circled in the air just overhead, and every time he caught sight of Shadow, he swooped at him with great, cruel claws spread to clutch him. Shadow dodged around the trunk of the tree. He was more angry than frightened, for his sharp eyes had spied a little hollow in a branch of the chestnut tree, and he knew that once inside of that, he would have nothing to fear. But he was angry clear through to think that he should be cheated out of that dinner he had been so sure of only a few minutes before. So he screeched angrily at old Redtail and then, watching his chance, scampered out to the hollow and whisked inside, just in the nick of time.

Chatterer, watching from the spruce tree, gave a great sigh of relief. He saw Redtail the Hawk post himself on the top of a tall tree where he could keep watch of that hollow in which Shadow had disappeared, and he knew that it would be a long time before Shadow would dare poke even his nose outside. Then, as soon as he was rested, Chatterer stole softly, oh, so softly, away through the treetops until he was sure that Redtail could not see him. Then he hurried. He wanted to get just as far away from Shadow the Weasel as he could. But Chatterer had learned his lesson.

Danny Meadow Mouse Wants a New Tail

DANNY MEADOW MOUSE sat on his doorstep with his chin in his hands, and it was very plain to see that Danny had something on his mind.

Now worry is one of the worst things in the world, and it didn't seem as if there was anything that Danny Meadow Mouse need worry about. But you know it is the easiest thing in the world to find something to worry over and make yourself uncomfortable about. And when you make yourself uncomfortable, you are almost sure to make everyone around you equally uncomfortable.

And what do you think was the matter with Danny Meadow Mouse? Why, he was worrying because his tail was short. Yes, Sir, that is all that ailed Danny Meadow Mouse that bright morning.

From *The Adventures of Danny Meadow Mouse,* Copyright, 1915, 1943, by Thornton W. Burgess.

You know, some people let their looks make them miserable. They worry because they are homely or freckled, or short or tall, or thin or stout, all of which is very foolish. And Danny Meadow Mouse was just as foolish in worrying because his tail was short.

Danny never had realized how short until he chanced to meet his cousin Whitefoot, who lives in the Green Forest. He was very elegantly dressed, but the most imposing thing about him was his long, slim, beautiful tail. Danny had at once become conscious of his own stubby little tail, and he had hardly had pride enough to hold his head up. Then he grew envious and began to wish and wish that he could have a long tail like his cousin Whitefoot.

He was so busy wishing that he had a long tail that he quite forgot to take care of the tail he did have, and he pretty nearly lost it and his life with it. Old Whitetail the Marsh Hawk spied Danny sitting there moping on his doorstep, and came sailing over the tops of the meadow grasses so softly that he all but caught Danny. If it hadn't been for one of the Merry Little Breezes, Danny would have been caught. And all because he was envious. It's a bad, bad habit.

All Danny Meadow Mouse could think about was his short tail. He was so ashamed of it that whenever anyone passed, he crawled out of sight so that they should not see how short his tail was. Instead of playing in the sunshine as he used to do, he sat and sulked. Pretty soon his friends began to pass without stopping. Finally one day old Mr. Toad sat down in front of Danny and began to ask questions.

"What's the matter?" asked old Mr. Toad.

"Nothing," replied Danny Meadow Mouse.

"I don't suppose there really is anything the matter, but what do you think is the matter?" said old Mr. Toad.

Danny fidgeted, and old Mr. Toad looked up at jolly, round, red Mr. Sun and winked. "Sun is just as bright as ever, isn't it?" he inquired.

"Yes," said Danny.

"Got plenty to eat and drink, haven't you?" continued Mr. Toad.

"Yes," said Danny.

"Seems to me that that is a pretty good-looking suit of clothes you're wearing," said Mr. Toad, eyeing Danny critically. "Sunny weather, plenty to eat and drink, and good clothes — must be you don't know when you're well off, Danny Meadow Mouse."

Danny hung his head. Finally he looked up and caught a kindly twinkle in old Mr. Toad's eyes. "Mr. Toad, how can I get a long tail like my cousin Whitefoot of the Green Forest?" he asked.

"So that's what's the matter! Ha! ha! ha! Danny Meadow Mouse, I'm ashamed of you! I certainly am ashamed of you!" said Mr. Toad. "What good would a long tail do you?"

For a minute Danny didn't know just what to say. "I—I—I'd look so much better if I had a long tail," he ventured.

Old Mr. Toad just laughed. "You never saw a Meadow Mouse with a long tail, did you? Of course not. What a sight it would be! Why, everybody on the Green Meadows would laugh themselves sick at the sight! You see, you need to be slim and trim and handsome to carry a long tail well. And then what a nuisance it would be! You would always have to be thinking of your tail and taking care to keep it out of harm's way. Look at me. I'm homely. Some folks call me ugly to look at. But no one tries to catch me as Farmer Brown's boy does Billy Mink because of his fine coat; and no one wants to put me in a cage because of a fine voice. I'm satisfied to be just as I am, and if you'll take my advice, Danny Meadow Mouse, you'll be satisfied to be just as you are."

"Perhaps you are right," said Danny Meadow Mouse after a little while. "I'll try."

Grandfather Frog Gets into Trouble

GRANDFATHER FROG has a great big mouth. You know that. Everybody does. His friends of the Smiling Pool, the Laughing Brook, and the Green Meadows have teased Grandfather Frog a great deal about the size of his mouth, but he hasn't minded in the least, not the very least. You see, he learned a long time ago that a big mouth is very handy for catching foolish green flies, especially when two happen to come along together. So he is rather proud of his big mouth, just as he is of his goggly eyes.

But once in a while his big mouth gets him into trouble. It's a way big mouths have. It holds so much that it makes him greedy sometimes. He stuffs it full after his stomach already has all that it can hold, and then of course he can't swallow. Then Grandfather Frog looks very foolish and silly and undignified, and everybody calls him a greedy fellow.

From *The Adventures of Grandfather Frog,* Copyright, 1915, 1943, by Thornton W. Burgess.

Now it happened that one morning when Grandfather Frog had a very good breakfast of foolish green flies and really didn't need another single thing to eat, who should come along but Little Joe Otter, who had been down to the Big River, fishing.

"Good morning, Grandfather Frog! Have you had your breakfast yet?" called Little Joe Otter.

Grandfather Frog wanted to say no, but he always tells the truth. "Ye-e-s," he replied. "I've had my breakfast, such as it was. Why do you ask?"

"Oh, for no reason in particular. I just thought that if you hadn't, you might like a fish. But as long as you have breakfasted, of course you don't want one," said Little Joe, his bright eyes beginning to twinkle. He held the fish out so that Grandfather Frog could see just how plump and nice they were.

"Chugarum!" exclaimed Grandfather Frog. "Those certainly are very nice fish, very nice fish indeed. It is very nice of you to think of a poor old fellow like me, and I—cr—well, I might find room for just a little teeny, weeny one, if you can spare it."

"Of course I can. But I wouldn't think of giving such an old friend a teeny, weeny one."

With that, Little Joe picked out the biggest fish he had and tossed it over to Grandfather Frog. It landed close by his nose with a great splash, and it was almost half as big as Grandfather Frog himself. It was plump and looked so tempting that Grandfather Frog forgot all about his full stomach. He even forgot to be polite and thank Little Joe Otter. He just opened his great mouth and seized the fish. Yes, Sir, that is just what he did. Almost before you could wink an eye, the fish had started down Grandfather Frog's throat head first.

Now you know Grandfather Frog has no teeth, and so he cannot bite things in two. He has to swallow them whole.

At first Little Joe Otter, sitting on the bank of the Smiling Pool, laughed himself almost sick as he watched Grandfather Frog trying to swallow a fish almost as big as himself, when his white and yellow waistcoat was already stuffed so full of foolish green flies that there wasn't room for anything more. Such greed

would have been disgusting, if it hadn't been so very, very funny. At least, it was funny at first, for the fish had stuck, with the tail hanging out of Grandfather Frog's big mouth. Grandfather Frog hitched this way and hitched that way on his big green lily pad, trying his best to swallow. Twice he tumbled off with a splash into the Smiling Pool. Each time he scrambled back again and rolled his great goggly eyes.

Little Joe was laughing so that he had to hold his sides, and he didn't understand that Grandfather Frog really was in trouble. He made such a noise that Spotty the Turtle, who had been taking a sun bath on the end of an old log, slipped into the water and started to see what it was all about.

Now Spotty the Turtle is very, very slow on land, but he is a good swimmer. He hurried now because he didn't want to miss the fun. At first he didn't see Grandfather Frog.

"What's the joke?" he asked.

Little Joe Otter simply pointed to Grandfather Frog. Little Joe had laughed so much that he couldn't even speak. Spotty looked over to the big green lily pad and started for Grandfather Frog as fast as he could swim. He climbed right up on the big green lily pad, and reaching out, grabbed the end of the fish tail in his beak-like mouth. Then Spotty the Turtle settled back and pulled, and Grandfather Frog settled back and pulled.

Splash! Grandfather Frog had fallen backward into the Smiling Pool on one side of the big green lily pad. Splash! Spotty the Turtle had fallen backward into the Smiling Pool on the opposite side of the big green lily pad. And the fish which had caused all the trouble lay floating on the water.

"Thank you! Thank you!" gasped Grandfather Frog, as he feebly crawled back on the lily pad. "A minute more, and I would have choked to death."

"Don't mention it," replied Spotty the Turtle.

"I never, never will," promised Grandfather Frog.

Jerry Muskrat Has a Fright

WHAT was it Mother Muskrat had said about Farmer Brown's boy and his traps? Jerry Muskrat sat on the edge of the Big Rock and kicked his heels while he tried to remember. The fact is, Jerry had not half heeded. He had been thinking of other things. Besides, it seemed to him that Mother Muskrat was altogether foolish about a great many things.

"Pooh!" said Jerry, throwing out his chest. "I guess I can take care of myself without being tied to my mother's apron strings! What if Farmer Brown's boy is setting traps around the Smiling Pool? I guess he can't fool your Uncle Jerry. He isn't so smart as he thinks he is; I can fool him any day." Jerry chuckled. He was thinking of how he had once fooled Farmer Brown's boy into thinking a big trout was on his hook.

Slowly Jerry slid into the Smiling Pool and swam over toward his favorite log.

From *The Adventures of Jerry Muskrat,* Copyright, 1914, 1942, by Thornton W. Burgess.

Peter Rabbit stuck his head over the edge of the bank. "Hi, Jerry," he shouted. "Last night I saw Farmer Brown's boy coming over this way with a lot of traps. Better watch out!"

"Go chase yourself, Peter Rabbit. I guess I can look out for myself," replied Jerry, just a little crossly.

Peter made a wry face and started for the sweet clover patch. Hardly was he out of sight when Billy Mink and Bobby Coon came down the Laughing Brook together. They seemed very much excited. When they saw Jerry Muskrat, they beckoned for him to come over where they were, and when he got there, they both talked at once and it was all about Farmer Brown's boy and his traps.

"You'd better watch out, Jerry," warned Billy Mink, who is a great traveler and has had wide experience.

"Oh, I guess I'm able to take care of myself," said Jerry airily, and once more started for his favorite log. And what do you suppose he was thinking about as he swam along? He was wishing that he knew what a trap looked like, for despite his boasting he didn't even know what he was to look out for. As he drew near his favorite log, something tickled his nose. He stopped swimming to sniff and sniff. My, how good it did smell! And it seemed to come right straight from the old log. Jerry began to swim as fast as he could. In a few minutes he scrambled out on the old log. Then Jerry rubbed his eyes three times to be sure that he saw aright. There were luscious pieces of carrot lying right in front of him.

Now there is nothing that Jerry Muskrat likes better than carrot. So he didn't stop to wonder how it got there. He just reached out for the nearest piece and ate it. Then he reached for the next piece and ate it. Then he did a funny little dance

just for joy. When he was quite out of breath, he sat down to rest.

Snap! Something had Jerry Muskrat by the tail! Jerry squealed with fright and pain. Oh, how it did hurt! He twisted and turned, but he was held fast and could not see what had him. Then he pulled and pulled, until it seemed as if his tail would pull off. But it didn't. So he kept pulling, and pretty soon the thing let go so suddenly that Jerry tumbled headfirst into the water.

When he reached home, Mother Muskrat did his sore tail up for him. "What did I tell you about traps?" she asked severely.

Jerry stopped crying. "Was that a trap?" he asked. Then he remembered that in his fright he didn't even see it. "Oh, dear," he moaned, "I wouldn't know one today if I met it."

Mother Muskrat called a convention at the Big Rock to try to decide what to do to keep Farmer Brown's boy from setting traps around the Smiling Pool and along the Laughing Brook. Everyone agreed to call in Grandfather Frog for advice.

Grandfather Frog cleared his throat. "Chugarum!" said he. "You must find all the traps that Farmer Brown's boy has set."

"How are we going to do it?" asked Bobby Coon.

"By looking for them," replied Grandfather Frog tartly. "When all the traps have been found, drop a stick or a stone in each. That will spring them, and then they will be harmless. Then you can bury them deep in the mud. But don't eat any of the food until you have sprung all of the traps, for just as likely as not you will get caught. When all the traps have been sprung, why not bring all the good things to eat which you find around them to the Big Rock and have a grand feast?"

So all day long they looked for traps and dropped sticks and stones into the traps and sprung them. Then they prepared for a grand feast of the good things to eat which Farmer Brown's boy had left scattered around the traps.

Johnny Chuck Finds the Greatest Thing

ANGER never stops to reason. It didn't now. Johnny Chuck hurried as fast as his short legs could take him toward the lone elm tree, and in his mind was just one thought — to drive a strange Chuck off the Green Meadows and to punish him so that he never, never would dare even think of coming back.

"I'll fix him! These are my Green Meadows, and no one else has any business here unless I say so! I'll fix him! I'll fix him!"

All his friends drew away from him, for they didn't want anything to do with anyone in such a frightful temper. But Johnny Chuck didn't even notice, and if he had he wouldn't have cared. That is the trouble with anger. It crowds out everything else, when it once fills the heart.

When Johnny had first seen the stranger, he had thought right away that it was the old gray Chuck with whom he had had such a terrible fight the day before and whom he whipped. Perhaps that was one reason for Johnny Chuck's terrible anger now, for the old gray Chuck had tried to drive Johnny Chuck off the Green Meadows.

But when he had to stop for breath and sat up to look again, he saw that it wasn't the old gray Chuck at all. It was a younger Chuck and much smaller than the old gray Chuck. It was smaller than Johnny himself.

"He'll be all the easier to whip," muttered Johnny, as he started on again, never once thinking of how unfair it would be to fight with one smaller than himself. That was because he was so angry. Anger never is fair.

But the stranger managed to keep out of his sight. Johnny Chuck was almost ready to give up, when he almost stumbled over the stranger, hiding in a little clump of bushes. And then a funny thing happened. What do you think it was?

Why, all the anger left Johnny Chuck. His hair no longer stood on end. He didn't know why, but all of a sudden he felt foolish, very foolish indeed.

"Who are you?" he demanded gruffly.

"I — I'm Polly Chuck," replied the stranger, in a small, timid voice.

After this, Johnny Chuck began to think about his clothes. Yes, Sir, he spent a whole lot of time thinking about how he looked and wishing that he had a handsomer coat. It seemed to Johnny that his own coat was so plain and so dull that no one would look at it twice.

"Oh, dear!" he sighed. "I don't see why Old Mother Nature didn't give me as handsome a coat as she did Reddy Fox."

Now this wasn't at all like Johnny Chuck to be discontented with his clothes. What was coming over him? He really didn't know himself. At least, he wouldn't have admitted that he knew. But right down deep in his heart was a great desire — the desire to have Polly Chuck admire him. Yes, Sir, that is what it was! And it seemed to him that she would admire him a great deal more if he wore fine clothes. You see, he hadn't learned yet what Peter Rabbit had learned a long time ago, which is that

Fine clothes but catch the passing eye;
Fine deeds win love from low and high.

Sometimes Polly Chuck would not notice him at all. Sometimes he would find her shyly peeping at him from behind a clump of grass. Then Johnny Chuck would try to make himself look very important, and would strut about as if he really did own the Green Meadows.

Sometimes she would hide from him, and when he found her she would run away. Other times she would be just as nice to him as she could be, and they would have a jolly time hunting for sweet clover and other nice things to eat. Then Johnny Chuck's heart would swell until it seemed to him that it would fairly burst with happiness.

Instead of wanting to drive Polly Chuck away from the Green Meadows, as he had the old gray Chuck, Johnny began to worry for fear that Polly Chuck might not stay on the Green Meadows. Whenever he thought of that, his heart would sink way, way down, and he would hurry to look for her and make sure that she was still there.

When he was beside her, he felt very big and strong and brave, and longed for a chance to show her how brave he was. She was such a timid little thing herself that the least little thing frightened her, and Johnny Chuck was glad that this was so, for it gave him a chance to protect her.

When he wasn't with her, he spent his time looking for new patches of sweet clover to take her to. At first she wouldn't go without a great deal of coaxing, but after a while he didn't have to coax at all. She seemed to delight to be with him as much as he did to be with her.

So Johnny Chuck grew happier and happier. He was happier than he had ever been in all his life before. You see, Johnny Chuck had found the greatest thing in the world. Do you know what it is? It is called love.

Mr. Mocker Makes New Friends

EVERYBODY was asking everybody else what the surprise could be which Unc' Billy had said he had for them. Billy Mink spoke of the matter to Little Joe Otter, and Little Joe Otter spoke of the matter to Jerry Muskrat, and Jerry Muskrat spoke of the matter to Sammy Jay, and right while he was speaking there came a shrill scream of "Thief! thief! thief!" from a thick hemlock tree near by, and the voice was just like the voice of Sammy Jay.

Sammy Jay became greatly excited.

"There!" he cried. "You heard that when you were standing right in front of me and talking to me, Jerry Muskrat. You know that I wasn't making a sound!"

Jerry Muskrat looked as if he couldn't believe his own ears. Just then the voice of Sticky-Toes the Tree Toad began to croak, "It's going to rain! It's going to rain! It's going to rain!" The voice seemed to come out of that very same hemlock tree.

From *The Adventures of Mr. Mocker*, Copyright, 1914, 1942, by Thornton W. Burgess.

Everybody noticed it and looked up at the tree, and while they were all trying to see Sticky-Toes, something dropped plop right into their midst. It was Sticky-Toes himself, and he had dropped from another tree altogether.

"You hear it!" he shrieked, dancing up and down, he was so angry. "You hear it! It isn't me, is it? That's my voice, yet it isn't mine, because I'm right here! How can I be here and over there too? Tell me that!"

No one could tell him, and Sticky-Toes continued to scold and putter and swell himself up with anger. But everybody forgot Sticky-Toes when they heard the voice of Blacky the Crow calling, "Caw, caw, caw!" from the very same hemlock tree. Now no one knew that Blacky the Crow had come to the party, for Blacky never goes abroad at night.

"Come out, Blacky!" they all shouted. But no Blacky appeared. Instead, out of that magic hemlock tree poured a beautiful song, so beautiful that when it ended everybody clapped their hands. After that there was a perfect flood of music, as if all the singers of the Green Forest and the Green Meadows were in that hemlock tree. There was the song of Mr. Redwing and the song of Jenny Wren, and the sweet notes of Carol the Meadowlark and the beautiful happy song of Little Friend the Song Sparrow. No one had ever heard anything like it, and when it ended everyone shouted for more. Even Sticky-Toes the Tree Toad forgot his ill temper.

Instead of more music, out from the hemlock tree flew a stranger. He was about the size of Sammy Jay and wore a modest gray suit with white trimmings. He flew over to a tall stump in the moonlight, and no sooner had he alighted than up beside him scrambled Unc' Billy Possum. Unc' Billy wore his broadest grin.

"Mah friends of the Green Forest and the Green Meadows, Ah wants yo'alls to know mah friend, Mistah Mockingbird, who

has come up from mah ol' home way down in 'Ol' Virginny.' He has the most wonderful voice in all the world, and when he wants to, he can make it sound just like the voice of any one of yo'alls. We uns is right sorry fo' the trouble we uns have made. It was all a joke, and now we asks yo' pardon. Mah friend Mistah Mockah would like to stay here and live, if yo'alls is willing," said Unc' Billy.

At first, when the little meadow and forest people were asked to pardon the tricks that Mr. Mocker and Unc' Billy Possum had played, a few were inclined not to. While they were talking the matter over, Mr. Mocker began to sing again that wonderful song of his. It was so beautiful that by the time it was ended, everyone was ready to grant the pardon. They crowded around him, and because he is good-natured, he made his voice sound just like the voice of each one who spoke to him. Of course they thought that was great fun, and by the time Unc' Billy Possum's moonlight party broke up, Mr. Mocker knew that he had made so many friends that he could stay in the Green Forest as long as he pleased.

But there were a lot of little people who were not at Unc' Billy Possum's party, because they go to bed instead of going out nights. Of course they heard all about the party the next morning and were very anxious indeed to see the stranger with the wonderful voice. So Mr. Mocker went calling with Ol' Mistah Buzzard, and they visited all the little meadow and forest people who had not been at the party. Of course, Mr. Mocker had to show off his wonderful voice to each one. When he had finished, he was tuckered out, was Mr. Mocker, but he was happy, for now he had made friends and could live on the edge of the Green Forest with his old friends, Unc' Billy Possum and Ol' Mistah Buzzard.

So he soon made himself at home and, because he was happy, he would sing all day long. And sometimes, when the moon was shining, he woke up in the night and would sing for very joy.

And as Ol' Mistah Buzzard said, "Mistah Mockah is the best loved of all the birds way down Souf."

Old Man Coyote Meets a Neighbor

IT WAS out at last. Digger the Badger had told Jimmy Skunk who it was that had so frightened the little people of the Green Forest and the Green Meadows with his terrible voice, and Jimmy Skunk had straightway sent the Merry Little Breezes of Old Mother West Wind over to the Smiling Pool, up along the Laughing Brook, through the Green Forest, and over the Green Meadows to spread the news that it was Old Man Coyote from the Great West who had come to make his home on the Green Meadows. And that night when they heard his voice, somehow it didn't sound so terrible. You see, they knew who it was, and that made all the difference in the world.

Digger the Badger, who had known him in the Great West where they had been neighbors, had told Jimmy Skunk what he looked like, and Jimmy Skunk had spread the news so that everybody would know Old Man Coyote when they saw him. So though each one knew that he mustn't give Old Man Coyote a chance to catch him, each felt sure right down in his heart that all he had to do was to be just a little bit smarter than Old Man Coyote, and he would be safe.

Of course it didn't take Old Man Coyote long to learn that he had been found out. He grinned to himself, stretched, and yawned, and then came out from his secret hiding place.

"I think I'll call on my neighbors," said he. "I hope they'll be glad to see me." Old Man Coyote grinned when he said this, for no one knew better than he did how very much afraid of him his new neighbors were.

But Reddy Fox is different. He dearly loves to tell how brave he is. He brags and boasts. But when he finds himself in a place where he is afraid, he shows it. Yes, Sir, he shows it. Reddy Fox has never learned to stand fast and look brave. When Reddy had first been told that the stranger with the voice which had sounded so terrible in the night was Old Man Coyote from the Great West, and that he had decided to make his home on the Green Meadows, Reddy had said: "Pooh! I'm not afraid of him!" and had swelled himself up and strutted back and forth as if he really meant it. But all the time Reddy took care, the very greatest care, to keep out of the way of Old Man Coyote.

Of course someone told Digger the Badger what Reddy had said, and Digger told Old Man Coyote, who just grinned and said nothing. But he noticed how careful Reddy was to keep out of his way, and he made up his mind that he would like to meet Reddy and find out how brave he really was. So one moonlight night he hid behind a big log near one of Reddy's favorite hunting places. Pretty soon Reddy came tiptoeing along, watching for foolish young mice. Just a little while before he had heard the voice of Old Man Coyote way over on the edge of the Old Pasture, so he never once thought of meeting him here. Just as he passed the end of the old log, a deep voice in the black shadow said:

"Good evening, Brother Fox."

Reddy whirled about. His heart seemed to come right up in his throat. It was too late to run, for there was Old Man Coyote right in front of him. Reddy tried to swell himself up just as he so often did before the little people who were afraid of him, but somehow he couldn't. "G-good evening, Mr. Coyote," he replied, but his voice sounded very weak. "I hear you've come to make your home on the Green Meadows. I-I hope we will be the best of friends."

"Of course we will," replied Old Man Coyote. "I'm always the best of friends with those who are not afraid of me, and I hear that you are not afraid of anybody."

"N-no, I-I'm not afraid of anybody," said Reddy. "Everybody is afraid of me." All the time he was speaking, he was slowly backing away, and in spite of his bold words, he was shaking with fear. Old Man Coyote saw it and he chuckled to himself.

"I'm not, Brother Fox!" he suddenly snapped, in a deep, horrid-sounding voice. "Gr-r-r-r, I'm not!" As he said it, all the hair along his back stood on end, and he showed all his great, cruel-looking teeth.

Instead of holding his ground as Jimmy Skunk would have done, Reddy leaped backward, tripped over his own tail, fell, and then scrambled to his feet with a frightened yelp, and ran as he had never run before in all his life. And as he ran, he heard Old Man Coyote laughing, and all the Green Meadows and the Green Forest heard it:

"Ho, ho, ho! Ha, ha, ha! Hee, hee, hee! Ho, ha, hee, ho! Reddy Fox isn't afraid! Ho, ho!"

Reddy ground his teeth in rage, but he kept on running.

A Discovery About Old Mr. Toad

IT WAS a beautiful spring evening. Over back of the Purple Hills to which Old Mother West Wind had taken her children, the Merry Little Breezes, and behind which jolly, round, red Mr. Sun had gone to bed, there was still a faint, clear light. But over the Green Meadows and the Smiling Pool the shadows had drawn a curtain of soft dusk which in the Green Forest became black. The little stars looked down from the sky and twinkled just to see their reflections twinkle back at them from the Smiling Pool. And there and all around it was perfect peace.

Jerry Muskrat swam back and forth, making little silver lines on the surface of the Smiling Pool and squeaking contentedly, for it was the hour which he loves best. Little Friend the Song Sparrow had tucked his head under his wing and gone to sleep among the alders along the Laughing Brook, and Redwing the Blackbird had done the same thing among the bulrushes. All the feathered songsters who had made joyous the bright day had gone to bed.

But this did not mean that the glad spring chorus was silent. Oh, my, no! No indeed! The Green Meadows were silent, and the Green Forest was silent, but as if to make up for this, the sweet singers of the Smiling Pool, the hylas and the frogs and Old Mr. Toad, were pouring out their gladness as if they had not been singing most of the departed day. You see, it was the hour they love best of all, the hour which seems to them just made for singing, and they were doing their best to tell Old Mother Nature how they love her, and how glad they were that she had brought back sweet Mistress Spring to waken them from their long sleep.

It was so peaceful and beautiful there that it didn't seem possible that danger of any kind could be lurking near. But Old Mr. Toad, swelling out that queer music bag in his throat and singing with all his might, was the first to see what looked like nothing so much as a little detached bit of the blackness of the Green Forest floating out towards the Smiling Pool.

Instantly he stopped singing. Now that was a signal. When he stopped singing, his nearest neighbor stopped singing, then the next one and the next, and in a minute there wasn't a sound from the Smiling Pool save the squeak of Jerry Muskrat hidden among the bulrushes. That great chorus stopped as abruptly as the electric lights go out when you press a button.

Back and forth over the Smiling Pool, this way and that way, floated the shadow, but there was no sign of any living thing in the Smiling Pool. After a while the shadow floated away over the Green Meadows without a sound.

"Hooty the Owl didn't get one of us that time," said Old Mr. Toad to his nearest neighbor, with a chuckle of satisfaction. Then he swelled out his music bag and began to sing again. And at once, as abruptly as it had stopped, the great chorus began again as joyous as before, for nothing had happened to bring sadness as might have but for the watchfulness of Old Mr. Toad.

"Why didn't you ever tell us before that you could sing?"
Peter Rabbit asked one day, as Old Mr. Toad looked up at him
from the Smiling Pool.

"What was the use of wasting my breath?" demanded Old
Mr. Toad. "You wouldn't have believed me if I had."

Peter knew that this was true, and he couldn't find any
answer ready.

Old Mr. Toad filled out his queer music bag under his
chin and began to sing again. Peter watched him. Now it just
happened that Old Mr. Toad was facing him, and so Peter looked
down straight into his eyes. He never had looked into Mr. Toad's
eyes before, and now he just stared and stared, for it came over
him that those eyes were very beautiful, very beautiful indeed.

"Oh!" he exclaimed, "what beautiful eyes you have!"

"So I've been told before," replied Old Mr. Toad. "My family always has had beautiful eyes. There is an old saying that every Toad has jewels in his head, but, of course, he hasn't, not real jewels. It is just the beautiful eyes. Excuse me, Peter, but I'm needed in that chorus." Old Mr. Toad once more swelled out his throat and began to sing.

Peter watched him a while longer, then hopped away to the dear Old Briar-patch, and he was very thoughtful.

"Never again will I call anybody homely and ugly until I know all about him," said Peter, which was a very wise decision.

Don't you think so?

Paddy the Beaver Wins an Argument

NOW, of all the little workers in the Green Forest, on the Green Meadows, and in the Smiling Pool, none can compare with Paddy the Beaver.

And when Sammy Jay reached the place deep in the Green Forest where Paddy the Beaver was so hard at work building a home, he didn't hide as had the little four-footed people. You see, of course, he had no reason to hide, because he felt perfectly safe. Paddy had just cut a big tree, and it fell with a crash as Sammy came hurrying up. Sammy was so surprised that for a minute he couldn't find his tongue. He had not supposed that anybody but Farmer Brown or Farmer Brown's boy could cut down so large a tree as that, and it quite took his breath away. But he got it again in a minute. He was boiling with anger, anyway, to think that he should have been the last to learn that Paddy had come down from the North to make his home

From *The Adventures of Paddy the Beaver*, Copyright, 1917, 1945, by Thornton W. Burgess.

in the Green Forest, and here was a chance to speak his mind.

"Thief! thief! thief!" he screamed in his harshest voice.

Paddy the Beaver looked up with a twinkle in his eyes. "Hello, Mr. Jay! I see you haven't any better manners than your cousin who lives up where I came from," said he.

"Thief! thief! thief! screamed Sammy, hopping up and down, he was so angry.

"Meaning yourself, I suppose," said Paddy. "I never did see an honest Jay, and I don't suppose I ever will."

"Ha, ha, ha!" laughed Peter Rabbit, who had quite forgotten that he was hiding.

"Oh, how do you do, Mr. Rabbit? I'm very glad you have called on me this morning," said Paddy, just as if he hadn't known all the time just where Peter was. "Mr. Jay seems to have gotten out of the wrong side of his bed this morning."

Peter laughed again. "He always does," said he. "If he didn't, he wouldn't be happy. You wouldn't think it to look at him, but he is happy right now. He doesn't know it, but he is. He always is happy when he can show what a bad temper he has."

Sammy Jay glared down at Peter. Then he glared at Paddy. And all the time he still shrieked "Thief!" as hard as ever he could. Paddy kept right on working, paying no attention to Sammy. This made Sammy more angry than ever. He kept coming nearer and nearer until at last he was in the very tree that Paddy happened to be cutting. Paddy's eyes twinkled.

"I'm no thief!" he exclaimed suddenly.

"You are! You are! Thief! Thief!" shrieked Sammy. "You're stealing our trees!"

"They're not your trees," retorted Paddy. "They belong to the Green Forest, and the Green Forest belongs to all who love it, and we all have a perfect right to take what we need from it. I need these trees, and I've just as much right to take them as you have to take the fat acorns that drop in the fall."

"No such thing!" screamed Sammy. You know he can't talk without screaming, and the more excited he gets, the louder he screams. "No such thing! Acorns are food. They are meant to eat. I have to have them to live. But you are cutting down whole trees. You are spoiling the Green Forest. You don't belong here. Nobody invited you, and nobody wants you. You're a thief!"

Then up spoke Jerry Muskrat, who, you know, is cousin to Paddy the Beaver.

"Don't you mind him," said he, pointing at Sammy Jay. "Nobody does. He's the greatest trouble-maker in the Green

Forest or on the Green Meadows. He would steal from his own relatives. Don't mind what he says, Cousin Paddy."

Now all this time Paddy had been working away just as if no one was around. Just as Jerry stopped speaking, Paddy thumped the ground with his tail, which is his way of warning people to watch out, and suddenly scurried away as fast as he could run. Sammy Jay was so surprised that he couldn't find his tongue for a minute, and he didn't notice anything peculiar about that tree. Then suddenly he felt himself falling. With a frightened scream, he spread his wings to fly, but branches of the tree swept him down with them right into the Laughing Brook.

You see, while Sammy had been speaking his mind, Paddy the Beaver had cut down the very tree in which he was sitting.

When Paddy begins work, he sticks to it until it is finished. He says that is the only way to succeed, and you know and I know that he is right.

Sammy wasn't hurt, but he was wet and muddy and terribly frightened — the most miserable-looking Jay that ever was seen. It was too much for all the little people who were hiding. They just had to laugh. Then they all came out to pay their respects to Paddy the Beaver.

Peter Cottontail Has Two Close Calls

FOR DAYS and days Reddy Fox had been trying to catch Peter, and Peter had had to keep his wits very sharp indeed in order to keep out of Reddy's way. Still, it didn't seem to worry Peter much. Just now he was hopping and skipping down the Lone Little Path without a care in the world.

Presently Peter found a comfortable spot close by a big rock. Underneath one edge of the rock was a place just big enough for Peter to crawl in — it was just the place for a nap. Peter was beginning to feel sleepy, so he crawled in there and soon was fast asleep.

By and by Peter began to dream. He dreamed that he had gone for a long walk, way, way off from the safe Old Briar-patch, and that out from behind a big bush had sprung Reddy Fox. Just as Reddy's teeth were about to close on Peter, Peter woke up. It was such a relief to find that he was really snug and safe under the big rock that he almost shouted aloud. But he didn't, and a minute later he was, oh, so glad he hadn't, for he heard a voice that seemed as if it were right in his ear. It was the voice of Reddy Fox. Yes, Sir, it was the voice of Reddy Fox.

Peter hardly dared to breathe, and you may be sure that he did not make even the smallest sound, for Reddy Fox was sitting on the very rock under which Peter was resting. Reddy Fox was talking to Blacky the Crow. Peter listened with all his might, for what do you think Reddy Fox was saying? Why, he was telling Blacky the Crow of a new plan to catch Peter Rabbit and was asking Blacky to help him.

Peter had never been so frightened in his life, for here was Reddy Fox so close to him that Peter could have reached out and touched one of Reddy's legs, as he kicked his heels over the edge of the big rock. By and by Blacky the Crow spoke.

"I saw Peter Rabbit coming down this way early this morning," said Blacky, "and I don't think he has gone home. Why don't you go over and hide near the Old Briar-patch and catch Peter when he comes back? I will watch out, and if I see Peter, I will tell him that you have gone hunting your breakfast way over beyond the big hill. Then he will not be on the watch."

"The very thing," exclaimed Reddy Fox, "and if I catch him, I will surely do something for you, Blacky. I believe that I will go right away."

Then the two rascals planned, and chuckled as they thought how they would outwit Peter Rabbit.

"I'm getting hungry," said Reddy Fox, as he arose and stretched. "I wonder if there is a field mouse hiding under this old rock. I believe I'll look and see."

Peter's heart almost stood still as he heard Reddy Fox slide down off the big rock. He wriggled himself still farther under the rock and held his breath. Just then Blacky the Crow gave a sharp "Caw, caw, caw!" That meant that Blacky saw something, and almost at once Peter heard a sound that sometimes filled his heart with fear but which now filled it with great joy. It was the voice of Bowser the Hound. Reddy Fox heard it, too, and he didn't stop to look under the big rock.

A little later Peter very cautiously crawled out of his resting place and climbed up where he could look over the Green Meadows. Way over on the far side he could see Reddy Fox running at the top of his speed, and behind him was Bowser the Hound.

"My! but that was a tight place," said Peter Rabbit, as he stretched himself.

Later, he had a bright idea. At least Peter thought it was, and he chuckled over it a great deal. What was it? Why, to follow the plan of Johnny Chuck and Grandfather Frog to avoid the cold, stormy weather by sleeping all winter.

So he curled up in an old house made a long time ago by Grandfather Skunk. He twisted and turned and tried to make himself feel sleepy. But soon he heard a noise that made him jump so that he bumped his head. He could hear claws scratching. Whoever it was, was digging. Digging! The very thought made every hair on Peter Rabbit stand on end.

With his heart almost in his mouth, Peter sprang out and started for the dear Old Briar-patch as fast as his long legs could take him. And then he heard a sound that made him stop suddenly and sit up.

"Ha, ha, ha! Ho, ho, ho! Hee, hee, hee!"

There, behind some bushes, Unc' Billy Possum, Bobby Coon, and Jimmy Skunk were laughing fit to kill themselves.

Then Peter knew that they had played a joke on him, and he shook his fist at them. But down in his heart he was glad, for he knew that he had learned his lesson — that he had no business to try to do what Old Mother Nature had never intended that he should do.

Poor Mrs. Quack Finds Happiness

FOR DAYS at a time Mrs. Quack hadn't had a full stomach because of the hunters with their terrible guns, and when just before dark that night she returned to the Smiling Pool, her stomach was quite empty.

"I don't suppose I'll find much to eat here, but a little in peace and safety is better than a feast with worry and danger," said she, swimming over to the brown, broken-down bulrushes on one side of the Smiling Pool and appearing to stand on her head as she plunged it under water and searched in the mud on the bottom for food. Peter Rabbit looked over at Jerry Muskrat sitting on the Big Rock, and Jerry winked. In a minute up bobbed the head of Mrs. Quack, and there was both a pleased and a worried look on her face. She had found some of the corn left there by Farmer Brown's boy. At once she swam out to the middle of the Smiling Pool, looking suspiciously this way and that way.

"There is corn over there," said she. "Do you know how it came there?"

From *The Adventures of Poor Mrs. Quack,* Copyright, 1917, 1945, by Thornton W. Burgess.

"I saw Farmer Brown's boy throwing something over there," replied Peter. "Didn't we tell you that he would be good to you?"

"Quack, quack, quack! I've seen that kind of kindness too often to be fooled by it," snapped Mrs. Quack. "He probably saw me leave in a hurry, and put this corn here, hoping that I would come back and find it and make up my mind to stay here awhile. He thinks that if I do, he'll have a chance to hide near enough to shoot me. I didn't believe this could be a safe place for me, and now I know it. I'll stay here tonight, but tomorrow I'll try to find some other place. Oh dear, it's dreadful not to have any place at all to feel safe in." There were tears in her eyes.

Peter thought of the dear Old Briar-patch and how safe he always felt there, and he felt a great pity for poor Mrs. Quack, who couldn't feel safe anywhere. And then right away he grew indignant that she should be so distrustful of Farmer Brown's boy, though if he had stopped to think, he would have remembered that once he was just as distrustful.

"I should think," said Peter with a great deal of dignity, "that you might at least believe what Jerry Muskrat and I, who live here all the time, tell you. We ought to know Farmer Brown's boy if anyone does, and we tell you that he won't harm a feather of you."

"He won't get the chance!" snapped Mrs. Quack.

Jerry Muskrat sniffed in disgust. "I don't doubt you have suffered a lot from men with terrible guns," said he, "but you

don't suppose Peter and I have lived as long as we have without learning a little, do you? I wouldn't trust many of those two-legged creatures myself, but Farmer Brown's boy is different. If all of them were like him, we wouldn't have a thing to fear from them. He has a heart. Yes, indeed, he has a heart. Now you take my advice and eat whatever he has put there for you. Be thankful, and stop worrying. Peter and I will keep watch and warn you if there is any danger."

I don't know as even this would have overcome Mrs. Quack's fears if it hadn't been for the taste of that good corn in her mouth, and her empty stomach. She couldn't, she just couldn't, resist these, and presently she was back among the rushes, hunting out the corn and wheat as fast as ever she could. When at last she could eat no more, she felt so comfortable that somehow the Smiling Pool didn't seem such a dangerous place after all, and she quite forgot Farmer Brown's boy. She found a snug hiding

place among the rushes too far out from the bank for Reddy Fox to surprise her, and then with a sleepy "Good night" to Jerry and Peter, she tucked her head under her wing and soon was fast asleep.

One day Mrs. Quack made a nest on the ground, a nest of dried grass and leaves, and lined it with the softest and most beautiful of linings, down plucked from her own breast. In it she laid ten eggs.

Then came long weeks of patient sitting on them, watching the wonder of growing things about her, the bursting into bloom of shy wood flowers, the unfolding of leaves on bush and tree, the springing up in a night of queer mushrooms, which people call toadstools, and all the time dreaming beautiful Duck dreams of the babies which would one day hatch from those precious eggs. She never left them save to get a little food and just enough exercise to keep her well and strong, and when she did leave them, she always carefully pulled soft down over them to keep them warm while she was away.

In due time, early one morning, Mrs. Quack proudly led forth for their first swim ten downy, funny Ducklings. Oh, those were happy days indeed for Mr. and Mrs. Quack.

Finally the Ducklings grew up, and when Jack Frost came in the fall, the whole family started on the long journey to the sunny Southland. I hope they got there safely, don't you?

Prickly Porky Is a Friend Indeed

WAY UP IN the top of a big poplar, the Merry Little Breezes found a stranger. He was bigger than any of the little meadow people, and he had long sharp teeth with which he was stripping the bark from the tree. The hair of his coat was long, and out of it peeped a thousand little spears.

The Merry Little Breezes hurried this way and that way over the Green Meadows and told everyone they met. Bowser the Hound heard about the stranger too, and went to the green forest to see him. My, how everybody did run from Bowser — everybody but the stranger.

"Bow, wow, wow!" shouted Bowser in his deepest voice.

But this stranger did not run away. Bowser was so surprised that he just stood still and stared. Then he growled his deepest growl. Still the stranger paid no attention to him. Bowser did not know what to make of it.

"I'll teach that fellow a lesson," said Bowser to himself. "I'll shake him and shake him and shake him until he hasn't any breath left."

From *The Adventures of Prickly Porky,* Copyright, 1916, 1944, by Thornton W. Burgess.

Bowser made a rush at him, and instead of running, what do you suppose the stranger did? He just rolled himself up in a tight ball with his head tucked down in his waistcoat. When he was rolled up that way, all the little spears hidden in the hair of his coat stood right out until he looked like a great chestnut burr. Bowser stopped short. Then he reached out his nose and sniffed at this queer thing. Slap! The tail of the stranger struck Bowser the Hound right across the side of his face, and a dozen of those little spears were left sticking there just like pins in a pincushion.

"Wow! wow! wow! wow!" yelled Bowser at the top of his lungs, and started for home with his tail between his legs, and yelling with every jump. Then the stranger unrolled himself and smiled, and all the little meadow people and forest folk who had been watching shouted aloud for joy. And this is the way that Prickly Porky the Porcupine made friends.

No one really knows who his best friends are until he gets in trouble. When everything is lovely and there is no sign of trouble anywhere, one may have ever and ever so many friends. At least, it may seem so. But let trouble come, and all too often these seeming friends disappear as if by magic, until only a few, sometimes a very few, are left. These are the real friends, the true friends, and they are worth more than all the others put together. Remember that if you are a true friend to anyone, you will stand by him and help him, no matter what happens. Sometimes it is almost worth while getting into trouble just to find out who your real friends are.

Peter Rabbit found out who some of his truest friends are when, because of his own carelessness, old Granny Fox caught him.

At Peter's screams of fright, Unc' Billy Possum scampered for the nearest tree, and Jimmy Skunk dodged behind a big stump. You see, it was so sudden that they really didn't know what had happened. But Prickly Porky, whom some people call stupid, made no move to run away. He happened to be looking at Peter when Granny caught him, and so he knew just what it meant. A spark of anger flashed in his usually dull eyes and for once in his life Prickly Porky moved quickly. The thousand little spears hidden in his coat suddenly stood on end and Prickly Porky made a fierce little rush forward.

"Drop him!" he grunted.

Granny Fox just snarled and backed away, dragging Peter with her and keeping him between Prickly Porky and herself.

By this time Jimmy Skunk had recovered himself. You know he is not afraid of anybody or anything. He sprang out from behind the stump, looking a wee bit shamefaced, and started for old Granny Fox.

"You let Peter Rabbit go!" he commanded in a very threatening way. Now the reason Jimmy Skunk is afraid of nobody is because he carries with him a little bag of very strong perfume which makes everybody sick but himself. Granny Fox knows all about this. For just a minute she hesitated. Then she thought that if Jimmy used it, it would be as bad for Peter as for her, and she didn't believe Jimmy would use it. So she kept on backing away, dragging Peter with her.

Then Unc' Billy Possum took a hand, and his was the bravest deed of all, for he knew that Granny was more than a match for him in a fight. He slipped down from the tree where he had sought safety, crept around behind Granny, and bit her sharply on one heel. Granny let go of Peter to turn and snap at Unc' Billy. This was Peter's chance. He slipped out from under Granny's paws and in a flash was safely behind Prickly Porky.

Reddy Fox Learns a New Trick

REDDY FOX lived with Granny Fox who was the wisest, slyest, smartest fox in all the country round. And now that Reddy had grown so big, she thought it about time that he began to learn the things that every fox should know. So every day she took him hunting with her and taught him all the things that she had learned about hunting, and all about the thousand and one ways of fooling a dog which she had learned.

This morning Granny Fox had taken Reddy over to the railroad track. Reddy had never been there before. Granny trotted ahead until they came to a long bridge. Then she stopped.

"Come here, Reddy, and look down," she commanded.

Reddy did as he was told, but a glance down made him giddy, so giddy that he nearly fell.

"Come across," said she, and ran lightly across to the other side.

But Reddy Fox was afraid that he would fall through into the water or onto the cruel rocks below. Granny Fox ran back to where Reddy sat.

From *The Adventures of Reddy Fox,* Copyright, 1913, 1941, by Thornton W. Burgess.

"For shame, Reddy Fox!" said she. "What are you afraid of? Just don't look down and you will be safe enough. Now come along over with me."

But Reddy Fox hung back and begged to go home and whimpered. Suddenly Granny Fox sprang to her feet, as if in great fright. "Bowser the Hound! Come, Reddy, come!" she cried, and started across the bridge as fast as she could go.

Reddy didn't stop to look or to think. His one idea was to get away from Bowser the Hound. "Wait, Granny! Wait!" he cried, and started after her as fast as he could run. When he was at last safely across, it was to find old Granny Fox sitting down laughing at him. Then for the first time Reddy looked behind him to see where Bowser the Hound might be. He was nowhere to be seen.

"Where is Bowser the Hound?" cried Reddy.

"Home in Farmer Brown's dooryard," replied Granny Fox dryly.

Reddy stared at her for a minute. Then he began to understand that Granny Fox had simply scared him into running across the bridge.

"Now we'll run back again," said Granny Fox.

And this time Reddy did.

Every day Granny Fox led Reddy Fox over to the long railroad bridge and made him run back and forth across it until he had no fear of it whatever.

"I don't see what good it does to be able to run across a bridge; anyone can do that!" exclaimed Reddy one day.

Granny Fox smiled. "Do you remember the first time you tried to do it?" she asked.

Reddy hung his head. Of course, he remembered that Granny had had to scare him into crossing that first time.

Suddenly Granny Fox lifted her head. "Hark!" she exclaimed.

Reddy pricked up his sharp, pointed ears. They heard the

baying of a dog, and the voice of the dog grew louder as it drew nearer.

"He certainly is following our track," said Granny Fox. "Now, Reddy, you run across the bridge and watch from the top of the little hill over there. Perhaps I can show you a trick that will teach you why I have made you learn to run across the bridge."

Reddy trotted across the long bridge and up to the top of the hill, as Granny had told him to. Then he sat down to watch. Granny trotted out in the middle of a field and sat down. Pretty soon a young hound broke out of the bushes, his nose in Granny's track. Then he looked up and saw her, and his voice grew still more savage and eager. Granny Fox started to run as soon as she was sure that the hound had seen her, but she did not run very fast. Reddy did not know what to make of it, for Granny seemed simply to be playing with the hound and not really trying to get away from him at all. Pretty soon Reddy heard another sound. It was a long, low rumble. Then there was a distant whistle. It was a train.

Granny heard it, too. As she ran, she began to work back toward the long bridge. The train was in sight now. Suddenly Granny Fox started across the bridge so fast that she looked like a little red streak. The dog was close at her heels when she started and he was so eager to catch her that he didn't see either the bridge or the train. But he couldn't begin to run as fast as Granny Fox. Oh, my, no! When she had reached the other side, he wasn't halfway across, and right behind him, whistling for him to get out of the way, was the train.

The hound gave one frightened yelp, and then he did the only thing he could do; he leaped down, down into the swift water below, and the last Reddy saw of him he was frantically trying to swim ashore.

"Now you know why I wanted you to learn to cross a bridge; it's a very nice way of getting rid of dogs," said Granny Fox, as she climbed up beside Reddy.

Sammy Jay Gets Caught

SAMMY JAY doesn't mind the cold of winter. Indeed, he rather likes it. Under his handsome coat of blue, trimmed with white, he wears a warm, silky suit of underwear, and he laughs at rough Brother North Wind and his cousin, Jack Frost. But still he doesn't like the winter as well as he does the warmer seasons because — well, because he is a lazy fellow and doesn't like to work for a living any harder than he has to, and in the winter it isn't so easy to get something to eat.

And there is another reason why Sammy Jay doesn't like the winter as well as the other seasons. What do you think it is? It isn't a nice reason at all. No, Sir, it isn't a nice reason at all. It is because it isn't so easy to stir up trouble. Somehow, Sammy Jay never seems really happy unless he is stirring up trouble for someone else. He just delights in tormenting other little people of the Green Meadows and the Green Forest.

From *The Adventures of Sammy Jay*, Copyright, 1915, 1943, by Thornton W. Burgess.

Dear, dear, it is a dreadful thing to say, but Sammy Jay is bold and bad. He steals! Yes, Sir, Sammy Jay steals whenever he gets a chance. He would rather steal a breakfast anytime than get it honestly. Now people who steal usually are very sly. Sammy Jay is sly. Indeed, he is one of the slyest of all the little people who live in the Green Forest. Instead of spending his time honestly hunting for his meals, he spends most of it watching his neighbors to find out where they have their storehouses, so that he can help himself when their backs are turned.

It was in this way that he had discovered one of the storehouses of Chatterer the Red Squirrel. He didn't let Chatterer know that he had discovered it. Oh, my, no! He didn't even go near it again for a long time. But he didn't forget it. Sammy Jay never forgets things of that kind, never! He thought of it often and often.

The snow was deep now, and things to eat were hard to find, but Chatterer the Red Squirrel wasn't asleep. No, indeed! Chatterer seemed to like the cold weather and was as frisky and spry as ever he is. And he never went very far away from that storehouse. Sammy Jay watched and watched, but never once did he get a chance to steal the sweet acorns that he had seen Chatterer store away in the fall.

"H-m-m!" said Sammy Jay to himself, "I must do something to get Chatterer away from his storehouse."

For a long time Sammy Jay sat in the top of a tall, dark pine tree, thinking and thinking. Then his sharp eyes twinkled with a look of great cunning, and he chuckled. It was a naughty chuckle. Away he flew to a very thick spruce tree some distance away in the Green Forest, but where Chatterer the Red Squirrel could hear him. There Sammy Jay began to make a great fuss. He screamed and screeched as only he can. Pretty soon, just as he expected, he saw Chatterer the Red Squirrel hurrying over to see what the fuss was all about. Sammy Jay slipped out of the other side of the spruce tree and without a sound hurried over to Chatterer's storehouse, where he helped himself to a breakfast of sweet acorns.

Now Chatterer had found a way to get all the corn he wanted by getting into Farmer Brown's corncrib, where was stored so much beautiful yellow corn. But what made him angry was to see Sammy Jay help himself to a few grains of corn from between the cracks in the walls of the corncrib.

Chatterer thought of a plan and chuckled wickedly. The next morning he was over in the corncrib bright and early, and stayed there until Sammy Jay arrived. Presently Sammy found a crack against which an ear of corn lay very close. He began to peck at it and pick out the grains. Chatterer stole over to it, taking the greatest care not to make a sound. Presently Sammy's black bill came poking through the crack. Chatterer seized it and held on.

Poor Sammy Jay! He was terribly frightened. He thought that it was some kind of a trap. He beat his wings and tried to scream but couldn't, because he couldn't open his mouth. Then Chatterer let go so suddenly that Sammy almost fell to the ground before he could catch his balance. He didn't wait to see what had caught him. He started for the Green Forest as fast as his wings could take him, and as he went he screamed with fright and anger. Chatterer chuckled, and his chuckle was a very wicked-sounding chuckle.

"I guess," said Chatterer, "that Sammy Jay will leave my corn alone after this."

Unc' Billy Possum Escapes

IT IS very startling to rush into your own storehouse, and run right into someone sleeping there as if he owned it. It is enough to make Happy Jack Squirrel lose his temper.

And it is very startling to be wakened out of pleasant dreams by having someone suddenly jump on you. It is enough to make Unc' Billy Possum lose his temper.

But Unc' Billy Possum is really very good-natured, and when he had gotten over the fright Happy Jack had given him and began to understand that he was in one of Happy Jack's storehouses, all his temper vanished, and presently he began to grin and then to laugh. Now it always takes two to make a quarrel, and one of the hardest things in the world is to keep cross when the one you are cross with won't keep cross, too. Happy Jack tried hard to stay angry, but every time he looked at Unc' Billy Possum's twinkling eyes and broad grin, Happy Jack lost a little of his own temper. Pretty soon he was laughing just as hard as Unc' Billy Possum.

From *The Adventures of Unc' Billy Possum*, Copyright, 1914, 1942, by Thornton W. Burgess.

"Ho, ho, ho! Ha, ha, ha!" they laughed together. Finally they had to stop for breath.

"What are you doing in my storehouse, Unc' Billy?" asked Happy Jack, when he could stop laughing.

Unc' Billy told him that he had gone off to get some fresh eggs for himself, but that Farmer Brown's boy had followed him, and how he had climbed there from another tree, so as to leave no tracks in the snow for Farmer Brown's boy to follow.

"But now Ah want to go to mah own home in the big hollow tree way down in the Green Forest, but Ah can't, on account of mah tracks in the snow," concluded Unc' Billy mournfully.

Happy Jack put his head on one side and thought very hard. "Why don't you stay right here until the snow goes, Unc' Billy?" he asked.

"Because Ah 'spects that mah ol' woman am worried most to death," said Unc' Billy, in a mournful voice.

"You're welcome to stay as long as you like, Unc' Billy," said Happy Jack. "You better stay right where you are, and I'll go tell old Mrs. Possum where you are."

"Thank yo'! Thank yo'! That is very kind of yo', Brer Squirrel. That will be a great help, fo' it will lift a great load off mah mind," said Unc' Billy.

"Don't mention it, Unc' Billy!" replied Happy Jack, and started off with the message to old Mrs. Possum.

Now, of course old Mrs. Possum was very much relieved when she heard that Unc' Billy was safe. But just as soon as she knew that he was safe, she forgot all about how worried she had been. All she thought of was how Unc' Billy had gone to get some fresh eggs to put in his own stomach and left her to take care of herself and eight baby Possums.

"Yo' tell Unc' Billy Possum that Ah done got other things to bother about more'n a worthless, no'count Possum what don' take care of his fam'ly," she said crossly, and hurried into the house to see that the eight little Possums were properly tucked in bed.

Happy Jack started back, and he knew perfectly well that when Unc' Billy got home, he would get a great scolding. Then all of a sudden Happy Jack thought of a way for Unc' Billy to get home without waiting until the snow melted away.

What do you suppose gave Happy Jack his idea? Why, a tiny little snowflake that hit Happy Jack on the end of his nose!

He hurried back to the hollow tree where Unc' Billy was hiding.

"Hello, Unc' Billy! You can go home tonight!" he shouted.

"What's that yo' say, Brer Squirrel?" he said. Ah don' see as the snow has gone away, and your tracks are powerful plain to see, and Ah makes bigger tracks than yo', Brer Squirrel. Ah do indeed."

"Just look up in the sky, Unc' Billy!" said Happy Jack.

Unc' Billy looked. The sky was full of dancing snowflakes. They got in his eyes and clung to his whiskers.

"Ah don' see anything but mo' snow, and yo' know Ah don' like snow!" he said. "What yo' driving at, Brer Squirrel?"

Happy Jack laughed. "Why it's just as simple as can be, Unc' Billy!" he cried. "Just as soon as it's dark, you start for home. It's going to snow all night, and in the morning there won't be any tracks. The snowflakes will have covered them all up."

Unc' Billy grinned. "Ah believe yo' are right, Brer Squirrel. Ah believe yo' are right!"

And Happy Jack was right, for Unc' Billy got safely home that very night, and the next morning, when Farmer Brown's boy visited the Green Forest, there wasn't a footprint to be seen anywhere.

So Unc' Billy Possum learned how easy it is to get into trouble and how hard to get out of it.

Bobby Coon Meets a Kind Boy

MORE THAN three fourths of the troubles that worry people are not real troubles at all. They are all in the mind. They are things that people are afraid are going to happen, and worry about until they are sure they will happen — and then they do not happen at all. Very, very often things that seem bad turn out to be blessings. All of us do a great deal of worrying for nothing. I know I do. Bobby Coon did when he took his strange journey which I am going to tell you about.

Farmer Brown and Farmer Brown's boy and Bowser the Hound had watched Bobby crawl out of his house. Of course, they had seen right away that something was wrong with Bobby, for he walked on three legs and held the fourth one up.

"The poor little chap," murmured Farmer Brown's boy pityingly. "That leg must have been hurt by a falling tree. We can't let him go off to suffer and perhaps die."

From *The Adventures of Bobby Coon*, Copyright, 1918, 1946, by Thornton W. Burgess.

Farmer Brown's boy ran forward and threw his coat over Bobby. In spite of Bobby's frantic struggles, Farmer Brown's boy gathered him up and wrapped the coat about him so that he could neither bite nor scratch. Bobby was quite helpless.

"I'm going to take him home, and make him quite comfortable," said Farmer Brown's boy.

Bobby could imagine all sorts of dreadful things, and he did. He was sure that when this journey ended the very worst that could happen would happen. It was the strangest journey he ever had known and it was the most terrible, though it needn't have been if only he could have known the truth.

Poor Bobby Coon! His broken leg pained him a great deal. Among the little people of the Green Forest and the Green Meadows, a broken leg or arm is a great deal worse than it is with us humans. We know how to fix the break so that Mother Nature may mend it and make the leg or arm as good as ever. But with the little people of the Green Forest and the Green Meadows, nothing of this sort is possible, and very, very often a broken limb means an early death.

So, though he didn't know it at the time, it was a very lucky thing for Bobby Coon that Farmer Brown's boy discovered that broken leg and wrapped him up in his coat and took him home. Bobby didn't think it was lucky. Oh, my, no! Bobby thought it was just the other way about. You see, he didn't know Farmer Brown's boy, except by sight. He didn't know of his gentleness and tender heart. All he knew of men and boys was that most of them seemed to delight in hunting him, in frightening him and trying to kill him.

When they reached the barn, Farmer Brown's boy put Bobby down very gently, but fastened him in the coat so that he couldn't get out. Then he went to the house and presently returned with some neat strips of clean white cloth. Then he

took out his knife and made very smooth two thin, flat sticks. When these suited him, he tied Bobby's hind legs together so that he couldn't kick with them. Then he placed Bobby on his side on a board and with a broad strip of cloth bound him to it in such a way that Bobby couldn't move. All the time he talked to Bobby in the gentlest of voices and did his best not to hurt him.

But Bobby couldn't understand, and to be wholly helpless, not to be able to kick or scratch or bite, was the most dreadful feeling he ever had known. He was sure that something worse was about to happen. You see, he didn't know anything about doctors, and so of course he couldn't know that Farmer Brown's boy was playing doctor.

Very, very gently Farmer Brown's boy felt of the broken leg. He brought the broken parts together, and when he was sure that they just fitted, he bound them in place on one of the thin, smooth, flat sticks with one of the strips of clean white cloth. Then he put the other smooth, flat stick above the break and wound the whole about with strips of cloth so tightly that there was no chance for those two sticks to slip. That was so that the two parts of the broken bone in the leg would be held just where they belonged until they could grow together. When it was done to suit him, he covered the outside with something very, very bitter and bad tasting. This was to keep Bobby from trying to tear off the cloth with his teeth. You see, he knew that if that leg was to become as good as ever it was, it must stay just as he had bound it until Old Mother Nature could heal it.

So Farmer Brown's boy played doctor, and a very gentle and kindly doctor he was, for his heart was full of pity for poor Bobby Coon. And Bobby soon got well and strong again.

Jimmy Skunk Uses His Perfume

REDDY FOX was close on Peter Rabbit's heels. He was running so fast that when Peter made a flying jump over a barrel, Reddy did not have time to jump too, and he ran right smack against that old barrel. He hit it so hard that the barrel started down a hill.

"As I live," Reddy Fox exclaimed, "I believe there was someone in that old barrel!" There was. In fact, Jimmy Skunk had curled up in there for a nap. Now Jimmy was awake, very much awake. He went over and over so fast that it made him dizzy. First he was right side up and then wrong side up, so fast that he couldn't tell which side up he was. And every time that old barrel jumped when it went over a hummock, Jimmy was tossed up so that he hit whatever part of the barrel happened to be above him.

From *The Adventures of Jimmy Skunk*, Copyright, 1918, 1946, by Thornton W. Burgess.

Now Reddy didn't know who was in the barrel. He just knew by the sounds that someone was. So he started down the hill after the barrel to see what would happen when it stopped. All the time Peter Rabbit was dancing about in the greatest excitement.

Down at the bottom of the hill was a big stone, and when the barrel hit this, the hoops broke, and the barrel fell all apart. There was Jimmy Skunk lying perfectly still. But presently Jimmy began to wave first one leg and then another, as if to make sure that he had some legs left. Then slowly he rolled over and got on to his feet.

Jimmy is one of the very best-natured little fellows in the world ordinarily. He minds his own business, and if no one interferes with him, he interferes with no one. But once he is aroused and feels that he hasn't been treated fairly, look out for him! And this time Jimmy was mad clear through, as he got to his feet.

He knew that an old barrel which has been lying in one place for a long time doesn't move of its own accord. He knew that the barrel couldn't possibly have started off down the hill unless someone had made it start, and he didn't have a doubt in the world that whoever had done it, had known that he was inside and had done it to make him uncomfortable. So just as soon as he had made sure that he was really alive and quite whole, he looked about to see who could have played such a trick on him.

The first person he saw was Reddy Fox. In fact, Reddy was right close at hand. You see, he had raced down the hill after the barrel to see who was in it when he heard the strange noises coming from it as it rolled and bounded down. If Reddy had known that it was Jimmy Skunk, he would have been quite content to remain at the top of the hill. But he didn't know, and if the truth be known, he had hopes that it might prove to be someone who would furnish him with a good breakfast. So, quite out of breath with running, Reddy arrived at the place where the old barrel had broken to pieces just as Jimmy got to his feet.

Now when Jimmy Skunk is angry, he doesn't bite and he doesn't scratch. You know Old Mother Nature has provided him with a little bag of perfume which Jimmy doesn't object to in the least, but which makes most people want to hold their noses and run. He never uses it, excepting when he is angry or in danger, but when he does use it, his enemies always turn tail and run. That is why he is afraid of no one, and why everyone respects Jimmy and his rights.

He used it now, and he didn't waste any time about it. He threw some of that perfume right in the face of Reddy Fox before Reddy had a chance to turn or to say a word.

"Take that!" snapped Jimmy Skunk. "Perhaps it will teach you not to play tricks on your honest neighbors!"

Poor Reddy! Some of that perfume got in his eyes and made them smart dreadfully. In fact, for a little while he couldn't see at all. And then the smell of it was so strong that it made him quite sick. He rolled over and over on the ground, choking and gasping and rubbing his eyes. Jimmy Skunk just stood and looked on, and there wasn't a bit of pity in his eyes.

"How do you like that?" said he. "You thought yourself very smart, rolling me downhill in a barrel, didn't you? You might have broken my neck."

"I didn't know you were in that barrel, and I didn't mean to roll it down the hill anyway," whined Reddy, when he could get his voice.

"Huh!" snorted Jimmy Skunk, who didn't believe a word of it.

"I didn't. Honestly I didn't," protested Reddy. "I ran against the barrel by accident, chasing Peter Rabbit. I didn't have any idea that anyone was in it."

"Huh!" said Jimmy Skunk again. "If you were chasing Peter Rabbit, where is he now?"

Reddy had to confess he didn't know. Jimmy looked this way and that way, but there was no sign of Peter Rabbit.

"Huh!" said he again, turning his back on Reddy Fox and walking away with a great deal of dignity.

Bob White Keeps His Home a Secret

THERE IS one who whistles, and it is such a clear and cheery whistle that it gladdens the hearts of all who hear it. A handsome little fellow is this whistler. He is dressed in brown, white, and black, and his name is Bob White. Sometimes he is called a Quail and sometimes a Partridge, but if you should ask him he would tell you promptly and clearly that he is Bob White, and he answers to no other name. All the other little people know and love him well.

Farmer Brown's boy loves him, not only for his cheerful whistle, but because he has found out that Bob White is a worker as well as a whistler, one of the best workers and greatest helpers on the farm. All the long day he works, and with him works Mrs. Bob and all the little Bobs, scratching up weed seeds here, and picking off bugs there.

You would think Bob White never had a thing in the world to worry about. But he does have plenty to worry about, and that is to keep his neighbors away from his nest.

Now Bob White wouldn't tell Peter Rabbit where his nest was hidden.

"I should think you would tell me where your home is," said Peter. "There ought not to be secrets between friends. I don't think much of a friendship that cannot be trusted."

"How would you feel, Peter, if harm came to me and my family through you?" asked Bob White.

"Dreadfully," declared Peter. "But do you suppose I would let any harm come to you?"

"No," replied Bob White soberly, "I don't think you would let any harm come to us if you knew it. But you've lived long enough, Peter, to know that there are eyes and ears and noses watching, listening, smelling everywhere all the time. Now supposing that when you were sure that nobody saw you, somebody did see you visit my house. Or supposing Reddy Fox just happened to run across your tracks and followed them to my house. It wouldn't be your fault if something dreadful happened to us, yet you would be the cause of it. You remember what I told you the other day, that there are some things it is better not to know."

Peter looked very thoughtful and pulled his whiskers while he turned this over in his mind. "That is a new idea to me," said he at last. "I never had thought of it before."

Bob White didn't feel that there was anything unfair in trying to fool his neighbors. He was doing it for love of shy little Mrs. Bob and their home, and for the kind of war that is always going on in the Green Forest and the Green Meadows. Of course, the little people who live there don't call it war, but you know how it is — the big people all the time trying to catch those smaller than themselves, and the little people all the time trying to get the best of the big people.

So Bob White felt that it was perfectly fair and right that he should fool those of his neighbors who were hunting for his home, and so it was. He would sit on a fence post whistling as only he can whistle, and telling all the world that he, Bob White, was there. Presently he would see Reddy Fox trotting down the Crooked Little Path and pretending that he was just out for a stroll and not at all interested in Bob or his affairs. Then Bob would pretend to look all around as if to see that no danger was near. After that he would fly over to a certain place which looked to be just the kind of a place for a nest, and there he would hide in the grass.

Just as soon as he disappeared, Reddy Fox would grin in that sly way of his and say to himself, "So that's where your nest is! I think I'll have a look over there."

Then he would steal over to where he had seen Bob disappear, and poke his sharp nose into every bunch of grass and peek under every little bush. Bob would wait until he heard those soft footsteps very near him, then he would fly up with a great noise of his swift little wings as if he were terribly frightened, and from a distant fence post he would call in the most anxious-sounding voice. Reddy would be sure then that he was near the nest and would hunt and hunt. All the time little Mrs. Bob would be sitting comfortably on those precious eggs in the nest in the weed patch close beside the Crooked Little Path, chuckling to herself as she listened to Bob's voice. You see, she knew just what he was doing.

It was the same way with Jimmy Skunk and Granny Fox and even Peter Rabbit. All of them hunted and hunted for that nest and watched Bob White and were sure that they knew just where to look. Jimmy Skunk wanted some of those eggs. Reddy and Granny Fox wanted to catch Mrs. Bob or be ready to gobble up the babies when they should hatch out of those beautiful white eggs.

As for Peter Rabbit, he wanted to know where that nest was just out of curiosity. So Bob White thought it best to fool Peter just as he did the others, and I think it was. Don't you?

Why Ol' Mistah Buzzard Doesn't Have a Nest

"YOU KNOW, Mistah Buzzard," said Peter Rabbit, "you haven't any nest and I thought there might be some reason, and so I came to you to find out."

"Ah'm not saying that this is the true reason why my family doesn't build nests," said Ol' Mistah Buzzard with a twinkle in his eyes, "but it is a story that has done been handed down to we-uns from way back at the beginning of things when the world was young. It was in the days when Granny and Granddaddy Buzzard, the first of mah family, lived, and eve'ybody was learning or trying to learn how to live. Yo' see, in those days nobody knew just what was best to do. Eve'ybody was trying to work out fo' himself what was best, and learning something every day. Of course, eve'ybody made mistakes, lots of them, Granddaddy and Granny Buzzard just like the rest, and it was because of one of these mistakes that they didn't have a nest like the rest of the birds.

"Yo' see, when the first nesting season came around and Ol' Mother Nature passed the word along fo' all the birds to prepare places fo' their aiggs and young, there were most as many ideas as there were kinds of birds. Each pair had their own idea of what a nest should be made of and where it should be put, and fo' a while there was a right smart lot of confusion.

" 'Ah tell you what,' say Granddaddy Buzzard to Granny Buzzard, 'we-uns don't know how to build a nest. Eve'ybody else has got a different idea, and Ah reckons we-uns haven't any idea at all. Ah don' see any sense in getting all heated up and tired out trying to do something when we-uns don' know what it is we want, so Ah reckons we-uns will just sit tight and watch our neighbors. When they done got their nests built we-uns will just go around and see which one we like best and which is easiest to build, and then we'll build one like it.' This suited Ol' Granny Buzzard and she wasn't a mite slow in saying so.

"Well, Granddaddy and Granny Buzzard just sat around and watched the other birds and said nothing, and looked wise. Ah reckons there was a terrible time building those first nests, and when they were all done Ah reckons none of them was much as nests go now. There was a right smart lot of fussing and worrying and quarreling, but Granddaddy and Granny Buzzard kept out of it and when anyone asked them where they were building their nest and what they were making it of, they simply looked wise as befo' and said nothing.

"Of course eve'ybody tried to make a powerful secret of where their nests were, but sitting around just watching, Granddaddy and Granny Buzzard found out where most of them were. They waited until the last of their neighbors had finished their nests and then they just went around looking at each to see how it was made and what it was made of. They found all kinds of nests, some made of sticks and some made of straw, and some made of mud, and some made of moss. Seemed like nary one of them just suited Granddaddy and Granny Buzzard. Anyway, they kept hoping that they would see one that would suit better, and so they kept a-looking and a-looking and a-looking. Granny Buzzard wanted her nest made out of something soft and comfortable, and Granddaddy Buzzard wanted it made of something it wouldn't be much work to find and less work to put together.

"So they couldn't make up their minds, and time went drifting along and drifting along, and first thing they knew eve'y last one of the other birds had a nest and aiggs, and here was Granddaddy and Granny Buzzard without even a place picked to build a nest. When Granddaddy Buzzard realized this he scratched his haid and began to look worried. Granny Buzzard scratched her haid and looked mo' worried.

" ' 'Pears like to me we-uns haven't got time to build a nest,' said Granddaddy Buzzard at last.

" 'Ah was thinking that ve'y same thing,' replied Granny Buzzard. 'If we stop to build a nest now, we-uns will be so late the season's gwine to be all over befo' we know it. Ah reckons Ah ought to be sitting on those aiggs right now.'

" 'Ah reckons that's right,' replied Granddaddy Buzzard, 'but fo' the life of me, Ah don' see what we-uns gwine to do about it.'

"Two or three days later Granny Buzzard called him to one side in a place where nobody was likely to come along and showed him two aiggs right on the ground. 'Ah reckons that is better than any nest,' said she. 'Nobody's gwine to look on the ground fo' aiggs, and if they do there's a powerful lot of ground to look over for two aiggs. The wind can't blow them out of a nest, and when they hatch the babies can't fall and hurt themselves. Ah'm gwine to sit right here until they hatch.'

"And ever since then the Buzzard family done got along without nests and have saved theirselves a powerful lot of work," concluded Ol' Mistah Buzzard.

And so we will leave Peter Rabbit and Ol' Mistah Buzzard, for this is the end of the book.

end

Bedtime Stories